To Luke
Enjoy mate
All the best

x

Victor
PUBLISHING
victorpublishing.co.uk

Woodchip Anaglypta And Nicotined Artex Ceilings

JB Barrington

My poems are like babies; beautiful to their creator
but to everyone else they're just silly and annoying

This book is the updated and revised edition October 2015

Published by Victor Publishing - victorpublishing.co.uk

ISBN: 9798563875968

Just a scrote done good from Salford

Pyjamas were once worn for bedtime
but they evolved into outside attire
no time for shame now the taste of fickle fame
is the flavour of the day to aspire
the paperboy's all but redundant
in a world where there's still work to do
the optimists are jaded now the stone clad has faded
down on worsley avenue
high on a wire hangs a shoe
see the gardens that we ran through
I'll come and call for you..........

Woodchip Anaglypta
And
Nicotined Artex Ceilings

JB Barrington

Contents

Poems **Pages**

The Blistering Sun

We've saved all year and the time is here
for a fortnights sun abroad
It won't be long before we're on that plane
and when it lands we'll all applaud
They'll bus us down to the local town
where the shops and bars are bigger
Where the olive skin trim from the gym
puts shame to my flaccid figure
The tanned up skin and whiter teeth
adorn the shimmering sands
I look like I've bathed in a bucket o' bleach
and just my teeth are tanned
And the bellies hang with the belly gang
over shorts that show short legs
We fall in love with the two for one
the sun and cheap cigarettes
And the English girl wants English beer
she wants Budweiser Becks and Stella
After egg & chips she grips her hips
to Flamenco for her fella
The observations form conversations
of who might be on them yachts
From the whites the blacks the thins the fats
the haves and the have nots
With studious looks we sift the books
at Carousel Karaoke Bar
Where every Mam and every Gran
thinks their horrible kid's a star
Tracy's up for the umpteenth time
she's murdering Adele
By 1am when the morning comes
she'll be gone like a bat out of hell
The northern folk crack smiles and jokes
with a sense of finesse and flair
Then the sound of the south with a massive mouth
pollutes what was a calm sea air
Sheila helps Joan try and work her phone
the stray cats get shooed away

As I burn my knees I catch a breeze
and try and make it last all day
To enjoy the heat with scolded feet
you'd have to be a Lizard
Drive me up the M62
drop me off in a Pennine blizzard
We've saved all year the time is here
so I'll plaster on fake smile
Where the water gun and the blistering sun
are fun........ for a while

You Had Me

You had me
When you first said hello
When the fervour in your eyes
Was all aglow
When the rapture and the passion
Was in full flow
You had me

You had me
With your beautiful face
That winsome smile
And your warm embrace
That elegant poise
And your enticing grace
You had me

You had me
With that sleek physique
The smell of Chanel
No5 on your cheek
A certain je ne sais quoi
Bereft of critique
You had me

You had me
You vicious twat
You fucked me over
And that's a fact
You kept the house
I got a flat
You had me

You had me
With all your bullshit lies
It's not you it's me
In your text replies
Whilst someone else
Got between your thighs
You had me

You had me
Over a fuckin' barrel
Stitched up like a kipper
You had me
Carol

You had me
Scriking every night
Listening to The Carpenters
By candle light
Without a pot to piss in
But you didn't give a shite
You had me

You had me
And now I wear my heart
Beneath a ripped sleeve
Since I fell apart
Now I only think of you
Whenever I fart
You had me

Letter From A Debtor

Woodchip Anaglypta and Nicotined Artex Ceilings

An old Salford docker
his name was Sid
said here's my advice son
for if you owe a few quid
he said write down the names
to whom you are a debtor
and each and every week
you should write them a letter
and in that letter
you politely explain
that things have got tight
and money is a strain
tell 'em each week
you can only afford
to pay one debt
after paying bread and board
tell em that's how it is
it's as simple as that
then tell 'em you'll put
all their names in a hat
tell 'em each week
when Friday comes round
you'll pull a name from the hat
and they'll be paid a few pound
but always remember
to tell 'em as their debtor
that if they keep sending
a threatening letter
they'll all stay unopened
upon the doormat
and you will not be putting
their names in the hat

The Precinct

Woodchip Anaglypta and Nicotined Artex Ceilings

The rain and the sleet
on the monolith concrete
would soak through that wide open space
benches for lovers
girls soon to be mothers
arms in anoraks wrapped in embrace
help the Police to beat yourself up
was where the marker pen met the profound
graffiti displays
like 'Jesus saves'
but Coppell gets it in on the rebound
slashes for grasses
and stitches for snitches
warned touts and spouts would meet their death
in a Ford Escort car
a skin digged his Ska
then in matt black paint he wrote NF
the object lessons
were scrawls of expressions
composed upon the cold precinct walls
and now I hurl my distaste
at the space they've replaced
with plastic and glass covered malls.

Me Mam Dunt Like To Text

Me Mam dunt like to text
The concept just leaves her well somewhat perplexed
She sez nobody talks I can't be doin'
The art of conversation's in rack and ruin
She said Margaret's got rid of her BT line
She dunt ring anymore she just text all the time
She sent one Tuesday saying Harry's had heart attack
Then I have to pay cos I ring her back
She gets a thousand free texts on contract ya know
Whereas I get nowt on this pay as you go
So if I wanna talk I have to call
Bleedin' textin' drives me up the wall
She sez I never asked this for this mobile son
As she works it with a finger instead of a thumb
Then she gets a message and she puts on her specs
It's Margaret, she rings her....cos she dunt like to text

Don't Look Down

When you focus in and concentrate
On those across the street
When you're quick to cast aspersions
On the vulnerable and weak
And when someones tongue just don't belong
To the language that you speak
When you feed off greed and believe what you read
Then grin yourself to sleep

When you carry round those leeches
Like golden chains around your feet
When you wave a flag then make a call
To shop a social cheat
When your nose is turned at those
With dog and blanket and beer can
I'll be venting my spleen at the killing machine
And not the downbeat poorer man

And when your TV shows
where tens of thousands died
You'll bitch and whinge
about those who smoke cigarettes
and takes their kids to school in taxi rides

When your views are cast upon the ones
Who fall down on their luck
When your furrowed frown has you looking down
When you really should be looking up
Up towards the ones that take the most away from you
And not towards the ones beneath
When they're simply making do

"before we blame the fruit on the ground we should first look at the tree that it fell from"

Greed Doesn't Know What The Meaning Of Peace Is

Sweet and innocent eyes
Lie still beneath night skies
A select few make
as children quake
Cos over life revenue overrides

As virtue turns to rags
Fire bombs fill body bags
Bereft of breath
with no life left
While the suits salute false flags

Echoes of why and what for
Form retorts to a world full of war
Blood soaked hands
send final demands
From a million miles offshore

Where puppetry meets pantomime
Where pounds kill pence and a dollar kills a dime
The young and the old
the clothed and unclothed
are innocent victims of war crime

Sons and daughters blown to pieces
Aunties and uncles nephews and nieces
But still the tills ring
cos cash is king
When greed doesn't know what the meaning of peace is

Adipose An' Affection

What's he supposed to say?
to "does me arse look fat in these?"
should he always safely say "no way!"
whilst the weight buckles the knees
when she's obviously gettin' bigger
does he tell her she's lookin' grand
should he tell her she's an hourglass figure
that could do wiv a little less sand
what's she supposed to say?
when his belly blocks the view of his cock
never one to want to cause dismay
she'll iron his shirt on a wok
what does it really matter?
should anyone really care?
if either or both grow fatter
as long as a love lives there

There's A Reason

There's a reason there's war where there's an oil supply
There's a reason we're the U.S. of A's ally
There's a reason there's over 600 channels on Sky
There's a reason why the hoi polloi must comply
There's a reason council tenants could buy their own home
There's a reason for easy credit and personal loans
There's a reason for the debt in the Eurozone
There's a reason for profit off all we once owned
There's a reason for every false flag in the press
There's a reason your pub's now a Tesco Express
There's a reason moderation turned into excess
There's a reason for each and every one of the protests
There's a reason the elite are allowed to succeed
There's a reason for folk wanting more than they need
There's a reason
and I've reasonable reason to believe
There's a reason and the reason's quite simple
It's greed

Me Myself And Greed

The banks they lend the money,
money that doesn't exist
The media serve up opiates,
to ensure we don't resist
Well I got bills and a mortgage mate,
is the prison they lock you in
To serve the system as robot & clone,
a slave to the powers within

Sit me down at the table,
where we all get equal shares
Don't sit me down at the table,
for the crumbs at the side of theirs
I'd rather die knowing,
I helped my fellow man
Instead of me myself and greed
never helping when they can

Everything we've paid for,
and everything we owned
Slowly sold for private gain,
from gas to phones to coal
They despise the idea of a welfare state,
they believe everything has a fee
Then the moment they break a finger nail,
they come to bleating to the likes of you and me

Sit me down at the table,
where we all get equal shares
Don't sit me down at the table,
for the crumbs at the side of theirs
I'd rather die knowing,
I helped my fellow man
Instead of me myself and greed
never helping when they can

The Dockers Christmas Eve

He shouts 'Christmas Eve
and all's crap'
He sez giz half o' best bitter
and half o' cider and black
He's thirty bob in his pocket
and ten park drive
Maureen's grabbed the mic
she's murdering I will survive
Flo feels the need to apologise
For Tommy's little stories
and their Tony tellin' lies
Sid swoons and stumbles
as Bing Crosby plays
Sheila shakes her head
sups her drink and walks away

And everyone borrows
from everyone else
And everyone drinks
to the health of themselves
Tales from the past
told through half empty glass
As the best time of year falls........
and falls apart on 'em

Billy plays the bandit
to the sound o' Slade
Charlie slams his pint down
cos his wife's not been paid
Stan stands and drinks
to the bar and the wall
Kev throws his coat to the floor
to fight 'em all
Johnny orders two dark mild
and a sherry for his Mam
The cellophane's off the sarnies
ya can't see their gobs for boiled ham

An' each drunken hug
is free love from top shelf
they leave as they came
with little to no wealth
happy thereafter
as tears follow laughter
as the best time of year falls.......
and falls apart on 'em

Eilleen shouts a line
and Barbara shouts for house
And on this eve before they leave
the winnings all get shared out
The landlord calls last orders
the last turn stands and sings
She sez everytime a bell rings
an angel gets it's wings
With a gulp o' stout her wings are out
she's flying down to that dancefloor
She's a new frock and she's ready to rock
to the song their Donna asked for

The young uns they all vacate
via taxis into town
Joe and Jean are still serving
under shutters half way down
Old Jack gets his coat ready
for when it's time to leave
He exhales one last song
and stands to sway along
for what will be his last Christmas Eve

She Holds His Hand

She holds his hand
He's no longer as strong as what once he could be
They fell in love in Salford 1953
She holds his hand
His legs have grown weak on his feet he's unsteady
She cleans him she feeds him she helps him get ready
She holds his hand
Never once does she wish to let go
Through the 65 years of blood sweat and tears
He's the most wonderful man she's ever known
She holds his hand
Just to make sure he's alright
She sings him to sleep with a sweet kiss to keep
And she holds his hand all through the night
She holds his hand
Just like she did before
Time got the best of those pains in his chest
She'll still hold his hand for evermore.

D'ya Wanna Cup O' Tea

I asked me Dad if he wanted a cup o' tea
an' a butty wi' some boiled ham
I said how many sugars d'ya have in ya brew
he said I don't know ask ya mam

I said mam I asked me dad if he wanted a brew
I asked him how many sugars he said to ask you
so how many sugars should I put in his cup
she said five but only stir two up

Sign For His Overtime

Woodchip Anaglypta and Nicotined Artex Ceilings

Pete punched his clock card
at five minutes to nine
at five past drop dead
on the production line
the foreman sighed
his workmates all cried
whilst stepping over him
to sign for his overtime

Soon To Be Oh So Superb

Where working folk would go to drink
After hard day on the docks
Now theatre claps to a different class
In chinos and stripes socks
Where a flock of fans fly from afar
To fawn upon a name
Nursing half an orange
For a photo chance with fading fame
Where tea stained über-trendies
Swap beers for the cup that cheers
Park up penny farthings
With the perfect Shoreditch beards
With E Cigs in beaks between both cheeks
Amongst the hemp and herbal tea
Where rock n roll faux socialism
Let the bands plug in and play for free
With tizer from tea pots and turn ups
Turned up towards the knee
Rolled up to reveal the half a calf
Of insufferable bourgeoisie
Where the oh so retro and and oh so vintage
Love all things oh so old
Combed up quiffs go sift the thrift stores
For all the dead folks clothes
It gets better and better at less and less
Turns more and more inside out
It's soon to be oh so superb
At fuck all and fuckin nowt

I've Never Seen A Chinese Copper

I've seen Boris Johnson support a tube strike
I've seen Eric Pickles on an exercise bike
I've seen a banker give his bonus to the poor and in need
I've seen capitalists casually castigate greed
I've seen Jamie Oliver scran a Burger King Whopper
But I've never seen a Chinese Copper

I've seen Katie Hopkins on Benefit Street
I've seen Morrissey in Morrisons shopping for meat
I've seen an Englishman buying a football club
I've seen a Tesco Express turned back to a pub
I've seen Miranda Hart say something witty
I've seen Alex Ferguson cheering for City
I've seen a builder building with his pants on proper
But I've never seen a Chinese Copper

I've seen Gary Neville give an unbiased view
I've seen the Daily Mail print a story that's true
I've seen Vladimir Putin waving rainbow flags
I've seen the Queen and Prince Philip carrying Aldi shopping bags
I've seen a Ryan Air flight take off on time
I've seen Tony Blair sent down for war crimes
I've seen me Gran going to bingo on a Raleigh chopper
But I've never seen a Chinese Copper

Posh Nosh

My Mrs took me out
To a Michelin star
It was all posh nosh
It was all Alan Carr (sorry, a la carte....or summat or something)
She said I know ya don't eat food
Ya can't spell or pronounce
But don't be showing me up
And take that tab out o' ya mouth
Shaking her head she said
I shoulda brought me Mam
You'd be better wiv a barm
And a quarter o' boiled ham
There was a look of disdain
In the maître d's eyes
And he pissed me right off
With his greeting of 'you guys'
I called the waiter to the table
I said he' are our kid
Is that right a bowl o' soup
For fifteen quid
He said sir this restaurant
Is Michelin star
I said I know it's posh nosh
It's all Alan Carr
I said you got a menu in English
This one's all in French
My Mrs was glaring
Wi' both fists clenched
I said there's rape on the menu
What's that all about
She said it's pronounced 'rapay'
Spanish Monkfish ya clown

I said I think I'll have the ménage à trois
Darling, how about you?
She said do not ask for a ménage à trois
You moron it's mange tout
You're a size 9 foot in a size 5 shoe
Square peg in roundest hole

With an undined unrefined palate
Of a fidgeting unfledged five year old (she said)
She ordered beetroot tart,
Wiv homemade goats' curd
I had a pork croquette wi' vinaigrette
Looked like a boiled turd
My Mrs was about to burst like tyre
I could see she was gonna explode
When I asked the waiter for a baked potato
He said there's a café just down the road
She said you're only happy under neon sign
Chomping at a leg o' mince
She dropped me off the kebab shop
I haven't seen her since

Things Me Mam Used To Say

Where did you lose it?
I don't know I can't find it that's why it's lost!
Don't be telling your Dad
How much them trainers cost
And don't be crossing that road
With your hood up at half past three
And if you fall off that wall and break your legs
Don't come running to me

You'll be feeling the back of my hand if you keep on mithering
I'll come over there and give you a clout
And if you keep on crying I'll be up them stairs
And give you something to really cry about
Get out of my sight you're getting on my nerves
I'm sick of you hanging around
I don't care who's at the door you're not going out
Until your tea's gone down

I've only just washed them jeans
I think you think I'm a Launderette
I've worked all week to pay for that food
So sit down and get it et*
Don't be turning on the tears these walls have ears
I got eyes in the back of me head
And if i have to shout you one more time
Get outta that bleedin' bed

If you're playing in that street don't give be giving cheek
And don't be messing about
Always remember no matter where you go or what you do
I'll always find out
Be careful on the main road son be careful what you do
There'll always be another bus
But there won't be another you!

** Salford slang for eaten*

The Day I Met You

My fears my doubts and pent up frustration
The years of pessimistic apprehension
My afflictions my anguish my fret and my wounds
Vanished the day I met you

My misery and misgivings my angst and my tears
My despair and don't care my growl and my sneers
My distress my disquiet my dark lonely mood
Vanished the day I met you

My gloomy my grim and my lonely isolation
My moaning my moping my sense of degradation
My pain and my sadness my bleak and my blue
Vanished the day I met you

My cheerful my chirpy my joyous jubilation
My merry my jolly my loud celebration
My glad and my glee and my wit and my woo
All came the day I met you

Now I embrace today and look forward to tomorrow
I feel true love and never feel sorrow
The mornings are bright with the light you bring through
Ever since the day I met you

A Nauseating Need For Nostalgia

The bootlicker click
the so sycophantic
will make haste for miles with stones in their shoe,
for a token photograph
that just makes us all laugh
whilst ignoring what's fresh and ignoring what's new,
a perpetual bask
in a distant past
whilst missing tomorrows made today,
suck off the outdated
spunk up when recreated
the same old albums on the same long play
a faded effervescence
from a sound of adolescence
no bands can place hands in the same river twice,
an expensive retrieve
of what once was prestige
when a nauseating need for nostalgia's the price

The Bingo Queue

I see they're goin' away again
Fourth time you know this year
I don't know how they do it ya know
Wi' what they spend in here on beer
An' I bet they got a night flight
So they can come and swank in here
They'll be sat in the vault wit' cases
In all their new holiday gear
I mean he dunt work and she's part time
It dunt half make you wonder
Me and Sid saved and saved for Salou
It did nowt but rain and thunder
I got him steak for his tea
Near on four pound thirty
Forty pence for a head o' lettuce
And her net curtains are filthy dirty
Police were at their door again
Nothing but a family o' crooks
I'd lock 'em all up and throw away the key
I wunt stand for it
Give us four books

Under Cold Eiderdown

Woodchip Anaglypta and Nicotined Artex Ceilings

It's a quarter to eight and the hedge trimmer's going
those privets just have to be neat
She rolls and turns over to face the woodchip
as the sound of the blades wake the street

She slips into slumber whilst catching a drift
as a bang cuts short her lie in
He's gone through the wire grits his teeth under breath
let the marital silence begin

It's a quarter to twelve and her hands warm her pockets
of her old and worn housecoat
And as they pass like ships in the night on the landing
she feels so cold and alone

Outside the sun is shining but inside there it rains
on a circumstance made man and wife
Not a glance exchanged or a single word spoken
as they lose another day in their life

It's a quarter to six and there's no appreciation
for the dinner she made hours ago
She holds on to her memories of music and dancing
he holds his ashtray and remote

It's a quarter to ten he shuts down the tele
she can hear every crack in his frown
They head on up the stairs and meet for one last time
in the dark under the cold eiderdown.

First Of The Ninth

Nobody ever asked us how we felt.....
just a crack and a smack of that leather belt.....
'you're going nowhere son, you're a waste of space'
from that blood red blood pressured horrible face...
and that place.......... that place........

....was where we first met when our Mams got off
And left us in a room where we cried
The first thing we said was..... 'can we go home?'
It was first of the ninth nineteen seventy five
It was the first day of the next twelve years
And we really didn't think we'd get through
And if we take off the time you'd spend in borstal
It'd be nine and half years for you.
The first few weeks were positively 'orrible
Learning to adjust to regimes
A shock to the system a smack round the face
Consumed by hordes of unperceived screams.
Our teacher looked like Lindsay Wagner
And the caretaker dressed like The Fonz
There were jigsaws and games and plastic toy trains
They weren't Hornby.... just wooden push along ones.
Progressing to carving our names on the desk
And laughing at my Timpsons two stripe
We both took a board rubber to the side of the head
But we just thought all that was alright
We both knew that was just the way it was
We didn't whinge tell tales or complain
None of it was any different for any other kid
On the estate from where we came
With fingers for ever shoved against lips
And sums that just sent us insane
Lines of 'I will behave and not be disruptive'
Wrote down..... and repeated.... again and again.
And again to the point where it drove us mental
Drove us to the point of despair
But I soldiered on always toeing the line
I had to, you didn't, ...you thought nobody cared
As boys we were thrust into sudden adolescence

And your antics never failed to impress
But each year that passed and each different class
Your presence became less and less.
Them teachers wouldn't talk about where you were
Or why you weren't sat by my side
It was all just as though you'd never existed
Or almost as if you had died.
Fast forward and on to the Secondary Modern
It was the first of the ninth eighty two
Your Mam had you go to the Catholic School
Something to do with a..... probation review
So I found my way and you found yours
Though yours weren't where I wanted to be
We'd meet once or twice and just compare trainers
I'd hear about your battles at half past three
I heard about the bank the shop and the garage
I heard about you sleeping in your Gran's garden shed
Strange how the stories just can't wait to find ya
And just like at Primary I'd just shake my head
See at Primary i thought it was me and you forever
Me and you against the world and all that
But two paths that were bowed met a fork in the road
And that's where we left everything we once laughed at
But you didn't last very long with the Catholics
Or more the Catholics didn't last long with you
They didn't take too kindly to pupils in class
Sitting at the back with a bag full of glue
Switch to a beautiful warm sunny morning
On the first of the ninth eighty four
The governors sighed and the P.T.A cried
As your simian walk brought you through the door
Right by my side was the chair I'd kept empty
At the start of each tedious term I'd beguile
You clocked it was a free...... then sat down beside me
With a nod.. and a wink.... and wry smile
See now your smile could open the securest of doors
And your charm would have 'em walk you right through
Your affable chatter and blag ladened patter

Had all the girls standing there in awe of you
You were lost in translation battered and bruised
So popular......... yet so very alone
You were the 'education systems Modus Vivendi'
But for me that was your one and only chance to atone
But you wouldn't have it you were off on your toes
You didn't even last a day
The chair to my side stayed tucked under table
And the days lost their names and the time slipped away
You were tarred with all blame bestowed a bad name
Some would say a crook......... a bad penny
But the fact was well known that you never robbed your own
You'd rob from the few and give to the many
The pensioners loved you at their Christmas party
For the Sherry they drank and the food that they ate
I'm not saying you were some kind of hero
You were stupid and foolish but you were my best mate
Your Mam told my Mam you were on a YTS
And I heard you'd only lasted four days
I heard the foreman said dig and you said 'what for 27 quid?'
Then you chased him round the site with the spade.
Adidas Dublin, München, Barrington Smash
Trimm Trabb and Forest Hills
You had 'em all and more besides
Long before them horrible pills
Long before the warehouse parties
In Blackburn Colne and Monroes
Way before the techno and acid all-nighters
That crack and that smack and that shit up your nose
This beautiful kid so cool and so clever
Was wrapped in an erratic and nebulous world
A world so obscure those inside don't even know it
Rolled up shoved away with no chance to unfurl
Then the light that burned so bright all those years
It just...... simply couldn't burn anymore....................
You danced your last dance, with a rope..... from a branch
It was the first of the ninth nineteen ninety four
It was the first day of the rest of our lives

That we'd have to spend without you
I'd sit and ponder the heavenly kingdom
Where hopefully you had arrived and checked into
Maybe you were organising pensioners parties
And smoking your fags with a piping hot brew
But then i don't believe in celestial bliss
And come to think of it neither did you
Grey clouds gave way to rays of sunshine
As the committal proceedings progressed
We watched as your Mam fell to her knees
On the day this world finally laid you to rest
And I think of you in my moments of silence
....I think of you in my moments of silence
.......I think of you in my moments of silence
..........I think of you in my moments of silence
The mad times the good times the memories instil
I believe you never ever stop loving someone
You either never did...........

...........or you always will.

Sick Note Mick

Sick note Mick has a walking stick
Cos the lager made his legs all sore
But he can't half run to get on Trap 1
When the hare starts running at Monmore
He nods and he winks and he says what he thinks
But never with intent to offend
His every divorce is par for the course
For every I do and each and every bitter end

He got married again to a girl called Elaine
She'd a face like a blistering piss pot
She drove the church with her Mam in a Transit van
Wearing nowt but a fur coat and flip flops
He met a girl called Stella she was really a fella
At a swingers night in Alderley Edge
He got a right shock went he went up her frock
And copped for a meat and two veg

He's in but he's out when the Provy's about
He'll peep around the curtain from within
The door'll be locked he'll say "let em fuckin knock
the paint will last longer than the skin"
He's a Broughton blagger with a Salford swagger
On the steps at Bexley Square
He's all love and light and he's proper alright
And if you ever need a friend he'll be there

He's got gambling debt and his only winning bet
Was a double up wi' two non-runners
He's had every blow that life can throw
So these days he stays under the covers
He's got rent arrears and his nine per cent beers
Fill the inside pockets of his coat
He coughs and he chokes on smuggled in smokes
His kids make paper aeroplanes with his sick notes
Through the air they soar from the fourteenth floor
From the flat in Thorn Court where they live
So if you're on Cross Lane and you find a paper aeroplane
See if it's a sick note for sick note Mick

When The World Was Young (and so was I)

That dance that glance
that suedehead stance
Them 2 tone covered ska tracks
them union flags
them bald scumbags
that culture that was hijacked
that toothless Jerry
that white Fred Perry
them blunt end skinny ties
those boots and braces
them shiny faces
when the world was young and so was I
That punch in Manny
that finger that fanny
that mad twat on our estate
those pots and pans
and that Lanky man's
mad wife at the garden gate
that council flat
that cricket bat
them beers under bright blue sky
them Farnworth fights
them City Lites when the world was young and so was I
That slag that blag
that three card bragg
that borrow 'til fridays pay day
them Chino slacks
them five pound jacks
those taxi runners round our way
that pulled out knife
that taken life
that scream in the night that cry
them wedge cut flickers
those tags on Kickers
when the world was young and so was I
Them play awaydays
those overnight stays
those Head bags full of Adidas

them second prize scars
them credit cards
and Mams that would believe us
them chippy teas
sat on settees
that love no money could buy
that smokers wheeze
those fives and threes
when the world was young and so was I
Them marching feet
in Borg elite
that crescendoing terrace cheer
them goals that missed
that first sweet kiss
them spokes to get first gear
them tooled up mobs
them mouthy gobs
that well deserved black eye
them scuffs and scrapes
those lucky escapes
when the world was young and so was I

Shake Of A Bucket By The Bargain Bin

The knock at the door
The rattle of a tin
The shake of a bucket
By the bargain bin

What pulls on the poor heartstrings
Also pulls on the poor people
From the cross at the top of the spire
To the wealth beneath the steeple

From local parishioners to PR practitioners
And the clipboard street sales pitch
To where the rich tell the poor to give their money to the poor
That were made poor by the rich

See the glossy ads and clever campaigns
For a celeb spawned heartfelt plea
See the vacant stares of millionaires
Here's the ad you won't see on TV...........

"We need to bomb another country
and we need your support
so dig down deep inside those pockets
and pledge what you can't afford"

It'll be a great day when our schools and hospitals
Have all the money they need
And Westminster holds its own fun run
To fund its war machine

See the more we give
The more they don't
And the more we will
The more they won't
And the more they don't
The more we do when cullled and coralled
In a catch 22

It's a chance to help for those in need
On a double edged sword or knife

They preach to the poor their recourse is a force
That offers a reward in the next life
"If I can help somebody as I pass along
then my living shall not be in vain"
While the hooray Henrys and Henriettas
Quaff the best champagne

Now if you put that pound back in your pocket
You're a skin-flint a non-caring soul
But misplaced caring to the poor and in need
Is as useful as no care at all

The knock at the door
The rattle of a tin
The shake of a bucket
By the bargain bin

Gone With The Ships
(a poem for Shelagh Delaney)

Raised letters on slugs of metal
all moulded in reverse
Punched through an ink soaked ribbon
for ten days worth of words

The smell of the grease paint the roar of the crowd
through Irish ancestral eyes
Then sealed in scenes on celluloid
under a smoke filled Salford sky

When a working class weren't represented
where another class graced the stage
The 'anyone for tennis' considered a menace
The young girl at eighteen years of age

The cover of class and of race and of gender
compelled to record and reflect what was real
You showed them a world they chose to ignore
spurred by those that were just too genteel

I'm oh so glad and I'm oh so grateful
for all them words you wrote
Putting northerners on the map you never once doffed a cap
and you spoke just like us ordinary folk

No narrative drool from a public school
with the stiffest of upper lips
That'd never stepped foot out of London
and never seen a pan o' chips

You perfectly scripted the impaired and afflicted
and those that never chose to have holes in their socks
A voice for the poor that is sadly no more
gone with the ships that sailed on the docks

Darts In The Wash House

Woodchip Anaglypta and Nicotined Artex Ceilings

My first bike was blue he painted it red
Police brought me home and sent me to bed
Stones on the track for a British Rail train
Fishing the boat shed in the cold pouring rain
Darts in the wash house round ours after tea
All the things I thought were always for me

A fresh lick of paint on a council front door
From the back of the van of the firm he worked for
Green hawthorn edges so pristine and neat
I still see them walking from work down the street
Darts in the wash house round ours after tea
All the things I thought were always for me

All my life I knew I loved you
And all we'd looked upon
You'll wake up there again tomorrow
To find that I have gone
Cos I'm moving on

So paint me a picture to take there with me
For once in a while to evoke memories
I say to the lovers and the friends that I made
We still got the trainers and the records we played
Darts in the wash house round ours after tea
All the things I thought were always for me

Problem Reaction Solution

They present you a **problem** covertly of course
So horrific to ensure you implore
They create and evolve an ostensible pretext
Then hatch their plans for made up war
The **reaction** desired sure will be acquired
When their media beams out the scenes
Hoodwinked eyes and public outcries
Oblivious to the agenda machine
From the 4th century scapegoat Christians
That Diocletian blamed for fire
To the modern day manufactured enemy
The elite orchestrate and empower
A sure-fire delusive **solution**
From the desired **reaction** they gleaned
And we all shake our fists unbeknownst to us it's
At a **problem** which never has been

4 & 5 Straight Forecast

The 4 dog takes the last bend
but the 5 dog's right behind
He's got 4 & 5 straight forecast
as they race towards the line
The 5 is closing on the 4
looks like it's gonna catch it
He shouts "Go on the 4 stay there the 5"
he screams "Don't go fuckin past it"
His heart beats fast as they flash past
the winning line side by side
He needs a win so he prays it's gone in
but once again he's denied
The resultant photo finish
declares it's 5 & 4
With a heavy frown the head goes down
the betting slip hits the floor
He's goes back to the board to point at the 4
does nowt but stand and curse it
He falls to his knees and desperately screams
"Why didn't I fuckin reverse it?"

The Vault

Pull us a pint o' Toby love
and take one for yourself
Me head's a shed I'm almost dead
cheers all the best good health
I never thought I'd see the day
when mine and hers roles were reversed
I was a proud working man before that dock closure plan
and now it's the wife that works
They paid me off and they paid me out
ten grand in the Gorton Tank
But I pissed it all against the wall
and what's left in me bank ain't worth a wank
How's it goin' how's your Dave?
no-one's seen him since he got barred
I always said he was a twistin' bastard
fiddlin' that fuckin' namecard
Alright Terry me old mucker
how's ya Mam everything alright?
I'm outta collar myself our kid
could do with a few days cash in hand like
I'm out on me Jack tomorra night
she's off down the bingo wi' their Mandy
Jimmy'll lend ya a couple o' quid
he's just dropped a ton on the bandit
How can that not be a fuckin' goal
how could that be disallowed?
I've just rang the wife to see what's for supper
she said I'm just warming it up for ya now
My lads run through women
like water through firemens hoses
They could all fall head first in a barrel o' shit
and still come out smelling o' roses
That's our kid on the day he got married
wiv his kipper tie and John Collier whistle
That's his mother in law there at the back
wiv a face like a fox lickin' shit of a thistle
That prick there sez he dunt like the Irish
or any foreigners black or brown

But he's supping Guinness he loves a curry
and he'll dance to that Tamla Motown
My lad's on his works doo
free food as much as he can sup
Alright Sheila, new fur coat
has your Graham had a fuckin' Yankee up?
Lung Cancer at forty six
he sez he ain't stopping smoking
Lovely fella seen him only last week
stood here wi' me laughing and joking
Right I'm off that's me 'til tommora
I'm going 'fore she gets in a mood
She'll be alright I'll stop at the chippy
she dunt moan if I come home wi' food
Two chips and gravy two buttered barms
and a 2p plastic fork
Wrap one up and leave one open
i'll eat mine while I walk

The Grapes Of Wrath

Now I don't know where they came from
Or where from they did sprout
But down in my rear for the last twenty year
I've had these things hanging out
I've tried a finger I've tried a fist
To try and push 'em back
I've tried every cream even red hot steam
Then my Mam said "Try Fiery Jack!"

When my courting first got a little intimate
And her roving hands were steered
To touch me beneath but she went right underneath
Then she froze like a ghost had appeared
I said they're merely veins draining the territory
Of the inferior rectal arteries
Well she puked down my throat and quickly grabbed her coat
And swiftly said ta-ra to me

I long for the days when these are all behind me
Just a tea towel holder down below
No anal twitching no hypnotic itching
No stinging after each time I go
I do hope you're not afflicted by these vicious Nazi Bastards
Cos trust me I know of no cure
Just a constant benign pharmaceutical line
Of products that cost more and more

One night outside Salford central station
I was scratching away to relax me
It was an absolute farce I wish I'd wiped my arse
Before I whistled for that fuckin taxi
It's not one bit funny it's no bleedin joke
So please please don't laugh
They're nowt but a pain and I wish I could abstain
From the dreaded grapes of wrath

 Trust A Fox Photography

 @TrustFox

Photos taken at the Manchester Academy 3rd May 2014

Peter O'Toole Illustrations

@peterotooleart

Follow JB on Facebook and Twitter

The Words Escape Me

@JB_Barrington

wordsescapeme1971

That win that place
That losing grace
That shake of the head
That sigh
Them rent arrears
Those Elephants ears
When the world was young
And so was I

Got a book in you?

This book is published by Victor Publishing.

Victor Publishing specialises in getting new and independent writers' work published worldwide in both paperback and Kindle format.

If you have a manuscript for a book of any genre (fiction, non-fiction, autobiographical, biographical or even reference or photographic/illustrative) and would like more information on how you can get your work published and on sale to the general public, please visit us at:

www.victorpublishing.co.uk

Printed in Great Britain
by Amazon